THE CLASSIC SERIES IS BACK!
CHOOSE FROM 15 POSSIBLE ENDINGS.

MOON QUEST

BY ANSON MONTGOMERY

CHOOSECO

$6.99 U.S.
$7.99 CAN

ISBN: 978-1-933390-26-0

Kids love reading
Choose Your Own Adventure®!

"I like that you only need to have one
book and you can read over and over
again without reading the same thing."
Shannon McDonnell, age 10

"I love it when books I read make me think.
In this book I felt like I was the one solving the
problems. I also liked the different endings."
Lainey Curtis, age 10

"*Choose Your Own Adventure* books are
like a maze. Everywhere you go you are
confronted with challenges and choices
about what to do about them."
Daniel Lee, age 11

"So many places to go from dying to
winning a battle or race. You get to be
the author and choose how it ends!"
Brooks Curran, age 11

Watch for these titles coming up in the
Choose Your Own Adventure® series.

Ask your bookseller for books you have missed
or visit us at cyoa.com to learn more.

MOON QUEST

BY ANSON MONTGOMERY

COVER AND INTERIOR ILLUSTRATED BY
VLADIMIR SEMIONOV

CHOOSE YOUR OWN ADVENTURE® CLASSICS
A DIVISION OF

CHOOSECO®
WAITSFIELD, VERMONT

Moon Quest ©2008 R. A. Montgomery
Warren, Vermont. All Rights Reserved.

Artwork, design, and revised text ©2008 Chooseco LLC,
Waitsfield, Vermont. All Rights Reserved.

Illustrated by: Vladimir Semionov
Book design: Stacey Hood, Big Eyedea Visual Design

For information regarding permission, write to:

CHOOSECO
P.O. Box 46
Waitsfield, Vermont 05673
www.cyoa.com

ISBN 10: 1-933390-26-3
ISBN 13: 978-1-933390-26-0

Published simultaneously in the United States and Canada

Printed in the United States of America.

0 9 8 7 6 5 4 3 2 1

To Rebecca

BEWARE and WARNING!

This book is different from other books.

You and YOU ALONE are in charge of what happens in this story.

There are dangers, choices, adventures, and consequences. YOU must use all of your numerous talents and much of your enormous intelligence. The wrong decision could end in disaster—even death. But, don't despair. At any time, YOU can go back and make another choice, alter the path of your story, and change its result.

Your home is a young nation on the Moon called the Tycho Colony. You live, work, and go to school beneath a glass dome facing the Earth. You are excited to be among the first humans living in Tycho Colony, but that doesn't mean it will be easy. Whether you scavenge the Far Side for signs of alien life or brave the Moon's dark inner tunnels-good luck to you!

The year is 2053, and you are living in the Moon. Your home lies underground cut from the cold rock. You have lived your whole life on Luna, the Moon's official name. Your parents were born on Earth, where humanity originated, but they joined an elite group of Moon Dwellers before you were born. Earthlings are stuck where they started; you are moving out to explore the universe.

Each year the colony in which you live, called the Tycho Colony, grows larger. More and more people come to live here permanently. Most of the new arrivals are scientists, but many are just ordinary people doing ordinary jobs. With over a hundred thousand people living on Luna, the economy has expanded beyond that of a mere research base. Also, the recently established Mars Colony has created a boom in the manufactured goods shipping business. The idea of declaring independence from Earth nations is growing as quickly as the population.

The Tycho Colony is made up of tunneled rock and large clear glass domes. Most people live in the old tunnels, but a few have moved into one of the main commercial centers in Big Dome. You don't understand why anyone would want to leave the tunnels; underground seems to you like the natural place to live.

Turn to page 2.

Unlike your parents, you try to stay out of Lunar politics. Both your parents are avid advocates for the Lunar Independence party, the party trying to gain self-rule for the Moon. Earthlings, they argue, have little understanding of the conditions on the Moon. To further complicate matters, over twenty independent Earth nations claim dominion over various aspects of the colony. Often one nation wants one thing, and another wants the opposite.

The Moon colonies would not survive without trade with the mother planet, and of course all your favorite television programs come from Earth. Even your parents like to watch Earth sports from time to time, especially if they get a chance to make fun of an Earthling burdened by gravity attempting to make a successful slam dunk in a basketball championship.

Right now, you're not thinking of politics or sports; you have other worries on your mind. Not only do you have to finish studying for your final school exams, you must also wrap up an important project for one of your jobs. You suppose that people on Earth would consider going to school, working two jobs, and living in an artificially constructed and maintained environment a little odd, but it is the only life you have ever known.

Go on to the next page.

Tomorrow June 22, is the first day of summer. You can hardly wait. Summer and winter are pretty much the same on the Moon, but the Earthling tradition of summer vacation from school continues on Luna. Looking through the meter-thick, extra-durable blister glass at the landscape outside, it looks pretty much the same all the time. You know of snow and trees with changing leaves from books and old movies. Before the polar ice caps melted on earth, one could always see some white on the blue planet, but when it's winter on Earth you can see white from snowfalls in their Northern Hemisphere.

Right now the sun is shining, but the only colors you see are black, white, and gray. There is no atmosphere to make the sky any other color than the black of outer space, and the sun burns and crackles with a life impossible to see from Earth. Since each Lunar day lasts about two weeks, there will be another ten days or so of sunlight where you live.

"What are you doing?" a voice asks.

Turn to page 4.

4

Turning around, you see your good friend and constant reality checker, Tamil.

"Nothing really. I was just thinking how living in the Moon makes us different."

"Well, snap out of it, dreamer," Tamil says with a smile.

"Don't you ever wonder about how your life might have been completely different?" you ask.

"Sure I do. But not when I'm busy cramming for calculus finals." Tamil sighs. "Some of us are just lowly mortals, not superbrains who can study and daydream at the same time."

Checking your wrist, you quickly glance at the watch that your Earthling grandfather sent you. The antique gadget actually has hands. It's so fragile that an accidental bump could easily destroy it, but you like it anyway. "Let's jet, or we'll miss the exam and have to spend all summer making it up."

Turn to page 7.

Tamil sighs again and without saying a word reaches out and grabs the right-hand towrope strung along the low ceiling of the passageway to school. Suddenly he is halfway down the corridor. When the colony was first established, there were no towropes in the passageways, and owing to the Moon's lower gravity, people often hit their heads on the ceilings. Dangling by your arm for a while does not strain you much when you weigh only twenty-five pounds. Your mass is still sixty-five kilos, both here and on Earth, but everything is about six times heavier on the big planet.

After six corridor switches, and four level changes, you make it to school. You look at your watch again. You still have three minutes to spare. You deposit your backpack in your locker and head toward the testing booths.

Each student takes his or her own individual booth and shuts the door. As soon as the door is closed, the computer simulation begins. Although you know that the person across from you is only a computer-generated hologram, you still find yourself reacting as if he were real.

"Good morning," a warm, deep male voice begins as the figure looks up from a stack of holo-graphic books. The face nods up and down slightly as the voice speaks. It is a typical man's face, but the hologram gives the skin a slightly greenish tint.

"Please prepare yourself for today's exercise. We will be discussing and evaluating your progress in learning the theories developed by Sir Isaac Newton."

Turn to the next page.

8

Two hours later, you feel like you've been interrogated by the secret police in a bad movie. At least now the ordeal is over. You think you did okay, but before you have time to settle down and collect yourself, you get your grade back.

"Congratulations. You have passed with a grade of 97 percent. You are eligible for highest honors and special placement in the Summer Scientific Corps."

"Let's go to the ponics park," Tamil says enthusiastically when you meet him outside the booths. "I need to see some green after that stressor. Emma said she was going there after her exam."

You agree that the Hydroponics Park is just the place to go. Even though you love the Moon and would not want to live anywhere else, sometimes you feel the need to get away from the artificiality of your man-made surroundings and the inhuman sterility of the Moon's surface. The park is a large, underground cavern where much of the Tycho Colony's food and oxygen are produced. Rows and rows of tomatoes, beans, corn, zucchini, and countless other vegetables reach upward toward the bright artificial sunlight burning in strips along the ceiling. The plants grow long and stringy in the weak gravity of the moon, but they taste pretty much the same as the vegetables imported from Earth.

Go on to the next page.

In one section of the cavern, an artificial stream runs along the ground and real trees reach up to the ceiling. Heavy vines hang from the canopy of trees—perfect for swinging from when the scientists and gardeners aren't looking. It's your favorite place to go when you need to relax. After you first brought Tamil there, he kept coming back and now just to bug you insists he discovered it. This is also the place where you both met Emma Byrnes. The three of you spend a lot of time in the ponics park.

Turn to the next page.

10

The trees are tall and thin. Branches leap out from the trunk in a dance of brown and green. You have seen pictures of trees on Earth, and they look stumpy and short compared to these wonders of good soil and light gravity. Strict quarantine controls have succeeded in keeping most common diseases and pests from harming the vegetation. Even in this part of the biggest hydroponics facility on the Moon, there are only about a hundred trees—mostly maples, spruce, and birch—but that is enough for right now.

"I don't care if I never meet a three-dimensional N-space that needs to have its volume discovered again," Tamil says as you plunk down at the base of a green-tinged poplar. "So come on, tell me, what was your grade, genius?"

"I passed," you say, as Tamil looks pleased thinking your silence means he got the better grade. Before he can pressure you any further, you're rescued by Emma's arrival.

"Hey, guys. Don't look so sad—summer's here!" she says as she plops down next to the two of you. "Did you flunk your exams or something?"

Go on to the next page.

"What are you going to do for the summer?" you ask your two friends, ignoring Emma's question.

"I dunno. I guess I'll help my dad carve out tunnels for more workspace. And I'm supposed to help fix those solar collectors over in the middle of the basin," Tamil replies. "How about you?"

"I'm not sure. My tour guide job has been pretty slow lately. No ships of tourists, and the geology lab hasn't yet told me if they want me to go on the exploration trip to the far side."

"The far side could be really cool," Emma says, "When will you find out?"

Turn to the next page.

"Hopefully today," you say as you hear a loud beep from Tamil's wrist com. Tamil punches in his access code to retrieve the information. He reads the display for a few seconds before turning to you. "It's for you," he says with a dramatic sigh. "I wish you would wear that beautiful Mark IV com your dad gave you last year. It seems like the only transmissions I get are for you."

"Enough of the pity party and more info," Emma says, leaning over to read the display.

Looking at the backlit display, you discover that there are actually two messages for you. One is from the geo lab, asking if you would like to come on the exploration mission. The other is from your boss, Al Cho, telling you that a special diplomatic ship from Earth is scheduled to arrive this afternoon. He wants you to guide the bigwigs around for a few days. Both messages contain apologies to Tamil for the infotrusion as well as pleas for immediate response.

A moment ago you had no idea what you were going to do this summer. Now you have to make a choice. You've never been to the far side, but it would also be exciting to show the diplomatic mission from Earth around. What should you do?

If you decide to go on the mission to the far side of the Moon, turn to page 14.

If you want to act as a tour guide, turn to page 30.

Normally you would jump at the chance to guide people—especially important diplomats—around some of your favorite spots, but the opportunity to go on an extensive research mission is too good to pass up. The mobile operation will be exploring some of the old volcanoes, mountains, and fault zones that give Luna its geographic personality and quirks. Even though you will be with professionals, you know there is a certain amount of danger. Working outside, far from any well-established habitation zone, you run the risk of injury, or worse. Still, all that you can think about is being involved in important research. There are also rumors about strange beings that live on the far side. Of course you do not believe them—most of the time.

"So you're going to the far side," Tamil says, stressing the word far.

"How did you know? I just made up my mind."

"Easy, that's what I would have chosen," Tamil says with a smile, "Besides I had a 50 percent chance of being right."

You head back to your home tunnels, making a mental list of what you will need to bring. The research equipment will be taken care of by the expedition manager. You get out your no-pressure suit. You'll need it for exploring Luna's surface. In a well-rehearsed routine, you carefully check the suit for holes and wear spots.

Go on to the next page.

The shiny material feels stiff and brittle, but you know it is durable. It will have to withstand the extremes of heat and cold that characterize Lunar weather and the jagged rocks that make up much of the landscape.

The entire suit ensemble is amazing, but the helmet is truly a piece of technological mastery. A polarized glass visor allows you to go from pitch-dark to glaring sunshine while retaining a perfect field of vision. Miniaturized controls for a wide range of functions nestle comfortably next to the wearer's head. The silvery material that forms the body of the suit is laced with control nodes connected to the helmet.

Turn to the next page.

All you have left to pack are toiletries and clothes. You also remember to get out your wrist com. Its directional finder, which is hooked up to a satellite network, will come in handy if you get lost on the Lunar plains. You also download your geology texts and a few books you have been meaning to read onto your wrist com. Now you just have to tell your parents.

"Oh, Mom," you start, "I just found out I've been invited to go on the expedition."

"But I thought the expedition wasn't for a while yet," she says. "And I was hoping you would talk to us before making a final decision."

"Yeah, but I have to go right now or I can't go at all. Oh, I got a 97 on my exam this morning."

Your mother's worried expression softens with pride. "Well, I guess that excellent grade buys you some freedom. You can go, but please be very careful."

Go on to the next page.

"Thanks, Mom!" You grab your bag and rush through the air lock to the main corridor.

The note from Dr. Nasir, the leader of the expedition, said to meet the team at the central staging station for transport. You travel through a maze of corridors and drop chutes. The departure point is next to the main air locks to the surface. When you arrive, you see men and women scurrying among huge piles of gear.

Looking out one of the viewports, you see the vehicle that will transport the team over the rugged Lunar territory. It looks vaguely insectoid, although you have only seen pictures of such creatures. The vehicle has rows of mechanical legs that are folded up in pairs on each of the three segments of the "bus." Normally the buses travel on huge spiked wheels, but even those can't manage some of the terrain you will encounter. When the bus reaches rocky terrain, the legs will slowly extend to slowly maneuver the rough landscape.

Moving through the chaos of people, instruments, and gear, you find Dr. Nasir and check in. You'd expected Dr. Nasir would be a stern forbidding academic, but the tall handsome woman greets you very warmly.

You locate a nice corner out of the way and try to make yourself comfortable. No sense getting in the way, you think as you shut your eyes.

"Wake up, the time has come," a voice booms into your dreams.

"What . . . where?" you mumble. "Oh—Doctor, are we ready?"

Turn to the next page.

Like many Earthlings on Luna for the first time, Dr. Nasir looks a bit disoriented, but her intelligence is obvious.

"I am fully prepared for this mission," Dr. Nasir tells you all firmly in a short opening speech. "I may be Earth-born, but I grew up in Egypt and am familiar with a climate you'd find surprisingly similar to the moonscape. In the desert, just as on the Moon, we study geologic subtleties that most people would lose patience with." Dr. Nasir's speech is short and informative, and you gather that although she is wise and very sharp, she lacks a sense of humor.

"We're ready," she says. "Let's get on board."

Putting your suit on and tucking your helmet beneath your arm, you prepare for the journey. Even though the bus is pressurized, everyone remains suited up at all times. In a crash, there's no time for dressing.

While you are trying to find where to sit, you hear a familiar voice. "How'd you end up on this mission?" Sarah Byrnes asks with a smile on her face. Emma's sister used to be shy around you, but that seems to have worn off.

"I just saw your sister at the ponics park," you say. "She didn't mention you were going on this trip."

"Yeah, well, I didn't know until right after exams myself, but here I am!"

"Good to see you, Sarah. I'm sure the expedition will be fun."

"Here, I'll help you get ready for the ride. I've done this a couple of times already," she says.

Turn to the next page.

Once you are strapped in, Dr. Nasir comes by and checks up on you. You're nervous, but you don't want her to know. "Everything's fine," you tell her.

"Oh, one more thing," says Dr. Nasir. "On this trip you'll have an opportunity to learn more about the specific aspects of each job. I'll be working with the analysis team, but you might want to learn more about the machines we use. Driving one of these rigs almost requires a degree itself, and operating the exoskeleton survey equipment is an art form. Let me know."

"Thanks, Doctor." This is going to take some thinking. You would like to work with Dr. Nasir. You know she could teach you an incredible amount in the lab. But the excitement of being in control of these powerful machines draws you as well.

If you decide to work with Dr. Nasir,
go on to the next page.

If you decide to learn how to run the machines,
turn to page 40.

When you tell Dr. Nasir you would like to work with her, she looks pleased. She motions for you to follow her to one of the storage rooms on the bus. You're not sure what all the secrecy is about, but you trust the doctor—although you're a little curious about her suddenly mysterious manner. Once in the storage room, Dr. Nasir checks the door to make sure that it is completely closed, then opens it quickly before shutting it tightly again. She sees you staring and gives a self-conscious laugh.

"Just making sure no one is listening in," she begins. "I'm really glad you chose to work with me, because now I can tell you what this expedition is all about. Otherwise I would have been forced to keep you in the dark."

"About what?" you ask.

"The city we are about to explore and study."

"What city? I thought we were going to the other colony."

"That's just it. We aren't studying one of our colonies. We're going to study one of the cities that was here before us." Dr. Nasir waits a few seconds for the importance of this information to sink in. "Our mission is to determine who, or what, made these cities and what happened to them."

Turn to the next page.

"Wow—you're talking about aliens from other planets, aren't you?" you ask with mounting excitement. This is turning into a much bigger adventure.

"Yes," the doctor answers soberly as though to caution your enthusiasm.

"Do you have any idea how old the ruins are?" you ask.

"No. All we know is that they are old. Countless centuries have passed since any living creature last walked along those streets. Since there is no atmosphere or water to wear things down, they tend to remain pretty much as they were, although they will show some signs of aging." The doctor looks at her watch. "But right now we have to prepare for tomorrow, and I'm sure that nothing we can imagine will come close to the reality of what we will see there."

"Thanks, Doctor. I'm glad I chose to work with you. This is very exciting."

Go on to the next page.

Throughout the day you can think of nothing but the alien city, and that night you dream about dusty relics coming to life before your eyes to reveal the secrets of the past. When you wake up the next morning, you aren't sure if the dreams were good or bad, but you do know that you miss your own bed and its regulated softness meter. Your head still feels fuzzy when the doctor comes looking for you, but you wake up quickly once she tells you that you're leaving for the ancient city site in just a few minutes.

Getting all the gear together for the day's expedition takes a while. Your suit feels loaded down with the gadgets that are strapped to it. You decide that this is what people on Earth must feel like all the time with gravity, and you're glad that you will be able to take the additional weight off at the end of the day.

Riding in a single-unit exploration craft, you and Dr. Nasir head toward the ancient city. For a long time you notice nothing out of the ordinary.

Turn to the next page.

Everywhere you look you see rocks and gray sand, but then you realize that something is odd about these rocks. They don't seem quite natural. It's as though they've been altered by someone— or something. A strange feeling overcomes you. You notice that the doctor has been glancing over at you frequently.

"So you feel it as well."

"I think so," you respond hesitantly.

"Good. Sensing the hidden is a valuable skill, but right now we are going to see something a bit more interesting." With that, the doctor stops the exploration craft. She exits the craft, bringing with her a sliver of rock. She slides this into a hole in one of the large rocks in your path—it fits like a key in a keyhole. A large hole, big enough to walk through, suddenly appears in the rock face.

"Follow me," the doctor says as she enters the hole. "You stay here in the entryway while I check out the rooms ahead."

"Okay," you say in a small voice.

The doctor leaves you in a room with polished stone walls that look like the inside of a geometry problem. You sit down to keep from getting disoriented, and when you lean back against one of the walls, another hole opens up across from you. The opening that the doctor went through seemed to lead to a room like the one you are in. In the next room, you see movement and colors, and the flash of metal gleaming in what looks like sunlight.

Turn to the next page.

This is definitely weird, you think. Somehow the swirl of movement doesn't scare you, although you aren't sure why. If this sort of thing happened back in Tycho, you would probably be running to the psychologist's station as fast as your feet could take you. You inch a little toward the hole. As you get closer, it becomes harder to clearly see what is going on.

"Doc . . . Doctor. Are you there?" you call softly over the radio, but you get no answer. "Come in, Doctor!" you yell. You feel a strong urge to check out this odd room, but you remember what the doctor told you. "Wait here," were her actual words, but underneath was the unspoken, "and don't do anything stupid."

The urge to just stick your hand into the hole is becoming irresistible. Even though the doctor told you to wait here, she would probably want you to check this out. This little light show seems to be more than oddly shaped rocks or the reflection of light. You don't know exactly where Dr. Nasir went, though, and the radios don't seem to be working. Maybe if you went partway through the hole, just to get a better view, you would be able to figure everything out. It seems like a good idea, but you are still uneasy.

If you decide to go looking for Dr. Nasir, turn to page 54.

If you choose to investigate the mysterious hole in the wall, turn to page 64.

There is nothing you can do to help John. You decide to stay with the expedition. Still, you feel pretty nervous as you watch the emergency runner start off across the silent dusty landscape. "Good luck, John," you whisper.

This time you stay in the bus during the ascent over the rim of mountains. You clench your fists every time there's a bump. Before lunch the bus is at the top of the rim, and you peer out the port window across the sharp landscape of the Moon. Since there is no real color to speak of, everything looks as though it is both near and far away at the same time.

Going down is even worse than going up, but at least it goes faster. Almost before you realize it, you are back on flat ground. The bus makes good time, and soon you reach the first site for analysis. A temporary camp is set up. You can feel the pressurization modules humming through the ground around the "tents."

The days pass, and many samples are taken and analyzed. You become very familiar with the machine that grinds the stones down to a perfectly smooth polish on one side. After the excitement of the first day, a pleasantly dull routine takes over.

The expedition spends about three days at each site. So many samples are taken that most have to be stored for later analysis back at the colony. By the time you reach the fourth site, you are almost a grizzled professional. That's when the excitement starts up again.

Turn the next page.

Everyone is busy working at their stations when Dr. Nasir lets out a yell. You see her jumping wildly up and down. Since she's usually so quiet and reserved, you decide to find out what is causing her excitement. By the time you get to her work area, a small crowd has gathered.

"So I placed the sample into the shielded pouch," you hear her say, "and then I thought nothing more of it. This was just a piece of radioactive rock, unusual on the moon, but not unheard of. I gave it no thought until I started working on the sample here, and that is when I realized what it must be." You feel the crowd straining to hear her conclusion. "It was a remnant of a nuclear explosion, a piece of radioactive slag created when the incident occurred. Judging from the half-life of the primary isotopes and the amount of decay, I would say that the explosion happened at least fifty thousand years ago."

"But that would be before humans ever set foot on Luna . . ." a voice starts before trailing off.

"Exactly," Dr. Nasir exclaims. "Someone, or something else besides humans, set off the explosion that created the crater in which we live. Now it looks like we'll need to send for some archaeologists too." She looks at you excitedly. "I'm glad you're onboard," she says. "We have years of exciting work ahead of us!"

The End

30

You decide to act as a tour guide for the diplomats from Earth. Often your tours consist of large groups moving to the Moon Colony, mostly scientists and their families. These new inhabitants do not tip well, but at least they ask intelligent questions. The other tour types are extremely wealthy or important people who tip well but make endless stupid comments. All in all, you prefer the scientists.

"What do you have for me, Al?" you ask as you walk into your boss's office. Al looks worried but manages a quick sigh and a smile. Everything seems slightly out of control in the normally calm workspace. Papers are strewn about, holographic displays run into and disrupt one another, and you see the half-eaten remains of a sandwich hiding under Al's desk.

"I'm glad you're here," he says. "When Ricardi canceled on me, I didn't know what I was going to do."

"You mean I was your second choice?" you ask, trying to sound offended.

Al looks up from his desk. "Of course I wanted you, but I knew that you had that geology job."

"Yeah, well, you were desperate, so I decided to help you out in your time of need," you say. "What's the big fuss about?"

"Just two days ago I found out that seven members of the Planetary Council will be arriving here to inspect the facilities and determine funding levels for the next decade."

Turn to the next page.

"Wow."

"That's right, wow. So as you can imagine, I've been spending all my time making sure everything goes smoothly while they are here. Your job is to entertain them and make sure that they appreciate the effort and cost that has gone into making this colony such a success. A lot is riding on this visit."

"I'm honored you want me to do the job," you say. "But don't you think that all this extra effort should be rewarded with, um . . . a little extra pay, Mr. Cho?"

Al looks at you as if you had refused him an air bottle on the Moon's surface, but finally a small smile breaks through. "This is extortion, but I suppose I should admire a young person who knows when to take advantage of a situation," he says. "However you will be rewarded with a raise only if you do an extraordinary job. If you don't, then both of us might be out of jobs." A worried frown appears on his face. "This job is all the more important because of increased tensions lately in the Planetary Council. I want someone I can trust if things get strange."

"What do you mean, 'strange'?"

"Oh, who knows what these crazy Earthlings will do. Anyway, I have to get back to work."

"When do I meet them?" you ask.

Go on to the next page.

"Two days from now at twelve in the main reception hall. Be prepared to show them anything they might want to see. You probably won't be doing any guiding that day. They will have just arrived from Earth, and they have to go through a long welcome ceremony," Al says with a sigh. "Don't be late."

"Gotcha, boss," you say as you leave. The assignment is definitely going to be more exciting than shuttling around a bunch of old billionaires, but you are more than a little nervous about the outcome of your mission.

Turn to the next page.

On the way home you think about what you will do once the delegation arrives. Normally all you have to do is show people around and make sure they don't do anything stupid, but this time you have to really sell what you're showing. You decide to visit the places in the colony that you think are particularly special, as well as refresh your memory about the more technological sites.

By the time the ceremony of welcome begins, you have crisscrossed the colony many times. From the fusion and fission energy-processing plants to the water-reclamation facility to the rope-flying dome, you have checked out everything that might be of interest. During the ceremony, which takes longer than you would have believed possible, you go through your mental checklist again and again.

At the end of the superintendent of hospitality's speech, the assembled crowd breaks into thunderous applause. You didn't think much of the speech, but you start to clap just as loudly as everyone else once you realize that the ceremony is over.

Looking up at the stage, you try to figure out what the seven representatives will be like. The three women and four men look perfectly ordinary except for their clothes, which might be practical on Earth but make them look uncomfortable and out of place on Luna. Then again, maybe it's more than their clothes that makes them look uncomfortable and out of place.

Go on to the next page.

After the ceremony, Al introduces you to the delegates. They all seem relieved to find out they don't have to start their tour until the next morning. You would like to get started because there is so much to show, but you realize that the tour members will be more favorable in their judgments if they are well rested.

Turn to the next page.

Early the next morning, you meet the delegates and prepare to show them around the colony. Merely getting used to the towropes in the tunnels takes them close to half an hour, and you realize that you will have to earn every cent of your pay. However, by the time you have shown the delegates around the hydroponics gardens and communal nursery, you get the feeling that they are enjoying themselves, and more importantly, are impressed by the efficiency and cleanliness of everything they see.

"All of this is most impressive," the delegate from Garania, an Earth country founded very recently, begins. "But I would most like to see the fission plant that allows you to synthesize your chemicals."

This is something you hadn't counted on. Although you are prepared to show them the power plant, you have never been to the experimental synthesizing facility yourself. Too dangerous to contemplate on Earth, where possible leaks could result in environmental damage, the synthesizing plant was the premier accomplishment of the colony. Because the plant is so important, it is off-limits to all except a few trusted workers. Normally you would simply tell the group that the plant is restricted, but you aren't sure if those restrictions apply to these planetary reviewers.

Turn to the next page.

Looking down at your wristwatch, you wish that you had worn your personal com unit. You move to the nearest wall phone and punch in the code to Al's office. When there is no answer, you realize you're on your own. Since your father works at the synthesizing plant, you know how to get there, and the credentials of the delegates should get you past the guards, but you're not sure that's the right thing to do.

What if something happens to the delegates? The plant is off-limits for safety reasons as well as security. Even small disturbances can upset the delicate synthesizing process.

"Can we go now, please?" the man from Garania asks.

If you agree to show the synthesis plant to the delegates, turn to page 50.

If you tell the delegates that you are not sure if the plant is safe right now and that you will take them to the surface of the moon instead, turn to page 62.

When you flip the switch of the emergency distress beacon, the display lights up. Every radio band in your suit sends out the message, and the locator beams your present position to the central computer at Tycho. Now all you can do is wait.

To pass the time, you think of your friends at home and the plans you made with them. You promise yourself that if you get out of this situation, you'll do all the things you never made time for before.

After a while, you feel as if your friends are actually there with you. Faces seem to float in front of yours, and you no longer feel so alone. But the feeling passes, and the truth of your situation seems even more terrible.

You watch as the beacon continuously sends its message. Surely someone must be just about to find you. Eventually you fall asleep. When you wake up, you see a flicker of movement from the corner of your eye.

The probe has been hard at work, and when it returns, water is its friend.

The End

40

You came on this mission to explore the lesser-known areas of the world you live in. Doing lab work would be like staying back in the Tycho Colony, but without the comforts. As these thoughts go through your head, you look out the forward viewport. The scratched blast-glass distorts your view, but you can see the wide gray plain of the crater floor. Fine dust is kicked up by the tires, but with no wind or air it settles down quickly, and you know that your tracks will stay there until something else comes this way.

After a while the mountains that form the crater's rim get closer and closer. The peaks are jagged and sharp. Dark shadows alternate with bright spots of brilliant reflection. Looking at the mountains, you do not see how the bus can possibly make it over them. You have seen some pretty amazing things in your life, feats that would be impossible on Earth: buggies being lifted over high crevices by flimsy-looking lines pulled by well-anchored men, and radio transmitters supported by towers a centimeter in diameter and over a hundred meters tall. No atmosphere and light gravity allow for many incredible possibilities, but you still are doubtful about making it over the mountains.

Still wondering about the upcoming ascent, you feel a tap on your shoulder. You turn to see an older man with a relaxed manner.

"Howdy," he says. "My name's John. I'm supposed to show you how we work some of this stuff."

Go on to the next page.

"Nice to meet you, John," you reply. "What stuff?"

"How we get this bus over the mountains, for one thing. I'll tell you, it's a sight to see."

"Okay," you say doubtfully. "What should I do?"

"Asking questions is a good start. Even if you think it sounds stupid, go ahead and ask. Lives have been lost by folks who don't ask enough questions," John tells you. "But right now, you just stay there. When the bus stops, in about ten minutes, we'll go outside and set up the winch."

The ten minutes seem to take forever, but eventually John comes back and tells you to get ready. You carefully align the contact points of your helmet. Once it's on, you bring up the displays, and everything seems to check out. A layer of air about a centimeter thick separates your skin from the suit. This internal air pressure acts as a buffer against falls and provides a few extra seconds if you have a puncture.

"Let's go," John says over the helmet radio system. He turns and heads to the air lock. You both get in. You hear the rushing of air being sucked out for reuse. Then you can't hear anything except your own breathing. Moving out carefully, you crawl down the ladder and jump the last five meters to the moon's surface.

Turn to the next page.

John lopes over to a big pile of gleaming metal machines. Grabbing one, he pulls out what looks like a huge gun and turns toward you. He kneels on one leg and starts adjusting it.

"This is the line gun," your helmet radio crackles. "I'm going to shoot a placement up to that ledge on the closest mountain." You see John point to the dark mountain that dominates the area directly in front of you. "Once we get up there, we'll pull the big winch up, and that will bring the bus up after us."

Turn to the next page.

"Okay," you say, more than a little nervous.

John stands, and before you realize it, he has shot a spike with a long metal cable trailing behind it. You see the spike crash into the side of the mountain and take hold.

"Give me your hand," John says. "Prepare to witness some of the wonders of a low-gravity lifestyle!" You put your gloved hand in his, and he hits the retract button. You both speed up the mountain to the ledge. You hold your breath the whole way up.

Once you are both safely on the ledge, John removes a winch and pulley set from his backpack. The metal gleams under the harsh sunlight. John uses the line from the winch to pull up an even larger pulley system and engine from the bus. You sit down on a flat rock and watch him set everything up. After an hour, he tells you that the show is about to begin. Waving his hand and speaking through his radio, he tells the people working at the bus to connect the steel line.

Turning toward you, John asks, "Want to throw the switch?"

You quickly answer yes. The lever to turn the winch on is small, but when you flip it, you feel the vibration through the soles of your boots. You look over the ledge and see the bus lift up on its rear tires as the tightening line pulls the front end up. Then you are able to see how the bus's insectlike legs work.

Turn to the next page.

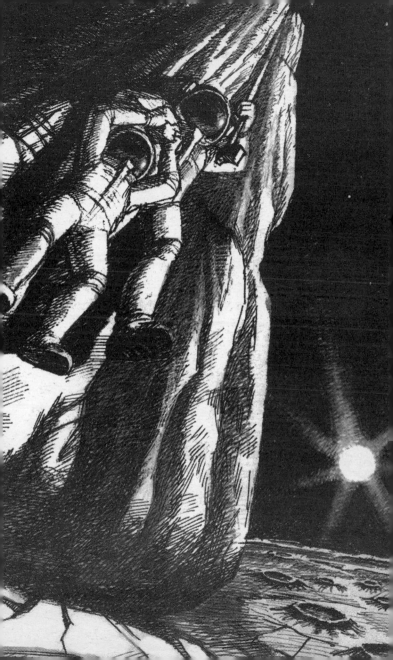

The legs extend and find holds in the rocky face of the cliff. You see the bus climb slowly but steadily up toward the ledge. You are amazed at the way its whole body moves, like something alive. "We got the idea from spiders," John says over the radio.

"I've seen pictures of spiders," you say, "but I've never seen a live one."

"Someday you should check out Earth," John says. "Right now, I want you to watch the bus and make sure the winch is turned off when it gets to the lip of the ledge. We don't want to pull the bus onto the ledge and have it bang into the rocks. I'm going to go up to that higher ledge and set up the second stage," he says, pointing to a rock outcropping. "Stay here."

"Okay."

John shoots another line out and is gone. You see him up above working on finding a secure spot. Turning your attention back to the bus, you watch its slow progress up the steep rocks. You're mesmerized by the slow movement of its legs as they climb with careful precision. Suddenly, a strong tremor shakes the earth. You throw your arms out instinctively, but you bounce forward and then are thrown facedown to the ground!

Turn to the next page.

A rock crashes next to you. You struggle to get back on your feet. You call to John and the bus on your radio, but there's no reply. The bus slowly continues its climb up the cliff face, but you see that a rock has hit its nose and dented it. What should you do? John has left another line gun behind, but he told you to stay here and wait for the bus. You don't know what will happen if you turn the winch off.

If you turn the winch off and go see if John is all right, turn to page 56.

If you decide to wait for the bus to make it to the ledge, turn to page 73.

There is no way you can risk hurting John any more. His experience would be of tremendous help, but you have to do this job on your own. You look over at his still form and get a chill. One of those rocks could have easily fallen on you.

The bus is still down there, and you have to make sure that no one gets hurt. Maybe if you shoot the cable just a little bit above where you are now, you can lower yourself down to the first ledge. This idea doesn't sound particularly attractive, but at the moment you don't have any others. Only a few hours ago you had never even seen a cable gun, and now the lives of many people depend on how well you use one.

Putting the hook into the nozzle of the gun, you aim and shoot in one smooth motion. You pull on the cable, testing it, and it appears to hold. You take the loose cable in your hands and slowly lower yourself. Since you are not being pulled by the miniature motor, there's no sudden jerking to upset your balance. If you weren't so scared, this might be fun.

Everything is going well, and that makes you nervous. One of the oldest sayings around is "Luna never lets it go the way it should." Even though you know that's just a silly saying, you have seen too many small accidents turn serious. As you kick out from the wall of rock, you feel the cable slip a little. It catches and then seems as sturdy as ever, but fresh fear grows within you.

Turn to page 61.

50

"We will have to take the special tunnel tube to the synthesis plant," you explain. "But you will not have to suit up for an outside expedition."

"Good. Let's get moving." You don't have to look to see who said that—you quickly recognize the voice of the pushy Garanian delegate.

"Okay," you say. "I'll get a locker at the end of the tunnel where you can put your bags until we get back." You hope that the guards won't ask to search the delegates if you have them put their belongings in the security lockers.

You arrive at the tube station after thoroughly confusing your tour with the many twists and turns of the interconnecting tunnels. You feel uneasy as you look at the armed guards standing by the portal. Seated at a desk is an even more imposing figure than the men with the guns. If you didn't know better, you would think he was some kind of robot.

"Good morning," the man says. "I'm afraid this area is off-limits to all nonworkers. You will have to leave now."

This is going to be harder than you expected, but you have to try. "I understand the ordinary restrictions," you begin. "But this is a special circumstance. These are delegates from the Planetary Council on a status report mission. Understanding the advances we have made in the field of synthesis is vital to their comprehending our society's industrial capabilities."

"I have had no word of this."

Turn to the next page.

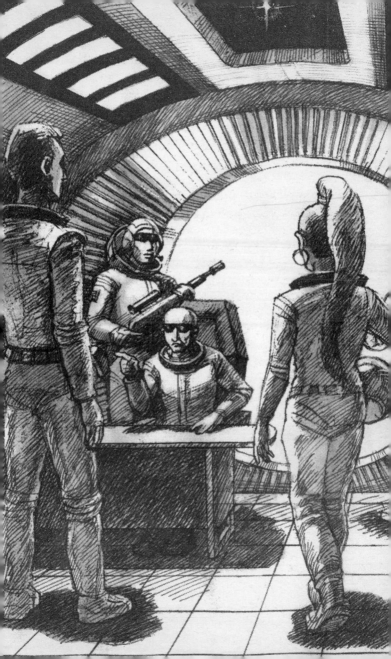

"If you want to call the colony director and get his approval, go ahead," you say, not knowing whether to hope he will call or not.

"Why don't I escort you on your tour," the guard says with a smile. "No need to bother the director."

Well that was easy, you think.

In moments you are in the tube, speeding toward the plant. Somehow, the man from Garania has managed to hold on to his pouch. You think about mentioning the pouch to the guard, but decide that going back to the station is not worth upsetting the delegate as they after all hold the financial future of the Colony in their hands. The tube makes sudden turns without warning, and you're thankful that there are straps for both hands.

Turn to page 120.

You decide to get out of this strange room before you do something that will get you into serious trouble. With one last look at the pulsing colors, you head off in the direction that the doctor took. The room you enter looks much like the last one, except there is definitely a different feeling to it.

Since you're not sure which way the doctor went, you decide to just make a blind choice. Taking the left-hand opening, you expect to see another room like the ones you have left. But as you move through the opening, it feels as though you are pushing against some thick membrane. Once you are all the way through, you hear a loud pop.

You look down at your external atmosphere gauge. Its sensors now indicate that the outside atmosphere is composed of 80 percent helium and 20 percent oxygen. This is not ideal for humans—helium makes human voices rise in pitch—but it's fine for sustaining life. *How did they manage to do that without an air lock?* you think.

Turn to page 99.

If John is hurt, immediate attention might be the only thing that will save him. You look down at the bus. All of its legs are securely wedged into crevices of rock. Trying the radio once more, you get ready to turn the winch off.

As you flip the lever into the off position, you feel another trembling through your body, but this one comes from the settling of the bus, not from a rockslide. Everything seems so still and silent you can hardly believe you are in the middle of an emergency. No time to think about that right now, though. You have to make sure John is all right without endangering everyone else.

Taking the spare line gun, you aim carefully, knowing you have to do it correctly the first time. You squeeze the trigger and hold your breath as the spike pulls the sturdy line behind it. The impact is silent, and you hope that the hooks are wedged in tightly. The last thing you want is to fall backward down a cliff onto sharp rocks. With one last look at the now-stationary bus, you hit the retract button.

Before you realize it, you are flying straight for a dark boulder. Reacting instinctively, you use your legs to push off it as soon as you get near. You scream, swinging out of control and losing your orientation. Pain flares in your shoulder as you collide with unyielding rock. You've never been more thankful that the no-pressure suit is so strong. This ascent is not nearly as smooth as when John was in charge, but at least you have stopped spinning.

Turn to the next page.

58

Almost before you know it, you are at the lip of the second ledge. You look over the top and see the remains of the rockslide. There is no sign of John. Clambering up, you search frantically, while calling John on your radio. You get no answer, but you do see something shiny buried in the rock pile. Now you are really scared.

"John," you whisper. "I hope you're okay." As you approach the rock pile, you realize that the shiny object is John's glove sticking out of the debris. Crouching down, you peer into the darkness where the rest of his body must lie. Luckily a large, flat rock lies directly over him, which may have shielded him from the crushing weight of the other rocks. However, you won't be able to pull him out because of the angle. You can't even tell if he is alive or not.

Go on to the next page.

Since there's no way to find out if John's okay, you will have to act as if he is. You look around for something to move the large flat rock and debris off him. You notice the winch beyond the rock-fall area. It looks as though one or two small stones might have hit it, but you think it might still work. No harm in giving it a shot.

Working carefully, you set up the winch so that it will lift the flat rock off John and away from him. The only thing you are worried about is rubble falling from above the rock. You don't want to crush John in the process of trying to save him.

With the hook firmly in place, you start the winch and watch as it slowly goes to work. The steel cable tightens, and the rocks shift and move. After a few minutes, you stop the winch. Crawling in carefully, you grab John's outstretched hand and pull. At first he feels stuck, but then you're able to slowly drag his body out.

Turn to the next page.

With John clear of the rubble, you can get a better idea of how badly hurt he is. Most of the lights on his external life-reading display have dipped into the amber section, but this just means he is hurt and unconscious, not in grave danger. You have a small med-kit with stimulants, but you're not sure if you should use them on him.

While you're taking care of John, you feel another shake. Your stomach cramps with fear as you turn toward the ledge. Looking down, you see the bus rocking against the walls. Even with the legs to support it, the constant shifting from the after-effects of the moonquake has slightly dislodged the winch mechanism, and the cable seems to be slowly playing out. You hope that the bus will just lower itself to the floor, but you're not sure that will happen.

Maybe if you used the stimulant, John would wake up and be able to tell you what to do. But you don't have much time. If you use the cable gun in reverse to rappel down to the first ledge, you might be able to switch the winch. The problem is that you never saw John use the gun to go down, and getting up to this ledge was almost more than you could handle. But you must make another life-or-death decision now.

If you try to wake John with the stimulant, turn to page 85.

If you decide to go down to the first ledge, turn to page 49.

Whoa!! Another little slip. This time you almost smashed into the rock face. You look down and see that you are about fifty meters from the ledge. The Moon may have weak gravity, but momentum and mass would still smash you to bits on the hard rocks. All you can see is dark shadow and burning sun. You're almost there—just a bit farther to go.

Twenty meters from the ledge you feel confident that you're going to make it, and the bus is still holding. Of course, just when you gain confidence and relax, the cable lets go. Your fall is dreamlike. Your arms flail as the unanchored metal rope comes sliding down toward you, and then you hit.

At first you think that you're paralyzed, but then the pain rushes in. Your vision starts to tunnel. Light and dark lose their meaning, but one thought holds your mind: You have to save the bus.

Crawling the two meters to the winch takes all your willpower, but you switch the lever to the correct position. After that, you pass out.

When you wake up in the hospital, you're confused until you see John's face. "Nice job, kid," you hear through a thick fog of pain. "You're a hero."

The End

"I'm sorry, but one of the procedures being done today at the plant is extremely delicate, and possibly dangerous," you tell the delegates. "Maybe tomorrow we can visit the plant. Right now I would like to give you a tour of the true wonder of our colony, our view of Earth." You hope this will appease the group, but you see some of them writing notes in their personal com units.

Getting everyone outfitted and prepped on the basics of outdoor survival techniques takes longer than you planned, but you are finally ready. You decide to take the group out in one of the midrange transports. Luxury is not one of the transport's attributes, but you find its ability to navigate over the roughest terrain truly impressive. Taking the transport a few kilometers out brings

you to one of the small mountain projections on the Plain of Tycho. The view there makes you feel closer to Earth than any other place on Luna, but even farther away from the water and life that it created.

The delegates move like bouncing balls with no guidance. As soon as you get them out of the air lock, you round them up and direct them into the transport. Riding to the mountain, which is nicknamed Trent's Peak after the colony's first director, you catch some of the delegates looking with disbelief at the piles of rock you casually drive over.

Turn to page 69.

You move across the chamber and cautiously stick your hand into the glowing opening. Before it is even a centimeter inside, a bright flash blinds you. Without knowing how, you realize that you are no longer in your no-pressure suit. When your eyes clear, you see something that you did not expect.

"Welcome," says a being seated in your father's favorite chair. You look around and see that you are in the study of your home. Even the burn marks on the cabinets are there, from when you played Moon-rock miner as a kid. But deep down you know that this is not really your home. You are dressed in your work uniform. Fear grips your stomach.

"Who are you?" you gasp.

"A figment," the man replies. You notice that his face is smooth and his eyes are deep gray, but his other facial features seem to constantly shift and change. "Your mind is creating this whole scene," he goes on, "in an attempt to make sense out of the impossible."

"What do you mean?"

"You are interfacing with our alien machines in a manner that makes you comfortable," the creature says as he leans forward. "I am the captured essence of our race."

"You mean the aliens who built this place?"

Turn to the next page.

"Yes," he replies. "We have been dead for a long time, but before our race died out, we created a method of passing on our legacy of achievement and failure. You are the first to receive it."

"Look, I just want to get out of here. This is not my home, and you tell me that not only are you an alien, you're a ghost!"

"I am not a ghost. My presence reflects the collective thoughts and feelings of my race. I am not alive, but I possess knowledge of what life was, and possibly will be."

Everything fades, and with no hint of movement, the alien stands in the middle of a white plain that goes on for what seems like forever. Your eyes hurt.

"Why are you doing this?" you ask.

"We do not want to have lived in vain. The wonders and terrors our society created are precious. If none know of them, they might as well never have happened. Your presence alone is worth the tremendous effort that went into my creation." The alien smiles.

"Great. Now can you put me back into my body? I promise—I'll remember you for the rest of my life."

The alien's face fades, then returns stronger than ever. "Your knowledge is redemption, but not fulfillment."

"What fulfillment are you talking about, and how do you expect me to help you with it?"

Go on to the next page.

"All we need is for you to accept the knowledge we gathered over our collective life span. We have no heirs. Our once lush and vibrant world is cold and dead. All that is left is our knowledge. All of our secrets will be made known to you. Not only will your technology benefit from the advances we struggled to achieve, but you will also gain a new viewpoint on your own lives and heritage. Only by passing on the knowledge of our triumphs and failures can we rest in peace."

"Why not someone else? I'm sure plenty of people would be glad to accept your offer. Let someone more powerful take your knowledge," you say, overwhelmed by the enormity of such a responsibility.

"Unfortunately, that is not the way the process works. Once our machines focused their attention on you, they were tuned to your thoughts, and yours only. We have only one chance—you."

"What if I say no?"

"That is your right, for our knowledge can only be taken as a gift. We cannot force you, and we would not, even if we had the means." The alien's face smoothes out. "You must choose whether our race is forgotten as a mystery or renewed in fellowship."

If you tell the alien that you're sorry but you do not want their knowledge inside your head, turn to page 80.

If you agree to receive the aliens' triumphs and failures, turn to page 104.

"I can't make the decision for everyone," you say.

"What decision?" Dr. Nasir asks.

You look up to see the doctor standing in the doorway. "Oh—nothing," you answer.

"Well, look what I found," she says, holding up some shiny objects. "I don't know what they are, but they are definitely important. I found them in a sealed room off the main corridor."

"They seem interesting," you tell her. What you do not tell her is that the objects are alien fin covers, worn when there was too much radiation. The closest human equivalent would be a rain jacket. "I wonder what they are," you muse.

"I have no idea," replies the doctor. "Maybe part of a ritualistic ceremony."

You nod and smile. "Just one of those mysteries that will never be solved."

The End

"This is a rugged place," someone whispers over the radio broadcast channel.

When you arrive at Trent's Peak, you suspect that everyone has forgotten about the synthesis plant. Stopping the transport, you carefully lead the delegates across the plain to the jumbled boulders that make up the base of the mountain. After a short hike, you glimpse the glowing green and blue globe of Earth behind the obscuring rock. Swirls of white shifting across its surface add movement to its serene beauty.

Turn to the next page.

The blazing sun falls on the distant globe, where the landmasses of the Americas are clearly visible. Gasps of appreciation escape into the radio intercom.

You let the delegates drink in the view for a couple of minutes. Just as you are about to begin your lecture on the usefulness of having a powerful observation facility, there is an explosion above you. A large chunk of rock hurtles downward. Chips of partially vaporized rock fly everywhere. You yell for everyone to get down.

"Is everyone all right?" you bark over the radio.

"What happened?" someone asks.

"That was a laser shot. Stay down. The next one might not miss."

As if on cue, another shot hits the rock above you. More debris rains down. You know that you have to get out of here. Whoever is shooting at you can simply work away at the rocks above and bury you all. The transport is only a few hundred meters away, but to get to it you have to cross the plain, where there is no cover.

Turn to the next page.

Who could be shooting at you? You know there are political tensions surrounding the delegates' visit—but attempted assassination? No time to think about it right now; you just want to make sure the shooters don't succeed in their mission.

You know there is an access hatch to one of the mining tunnels a few kilometers along the ridge that culminates in Trent's Peak. The problem is, you have no idea where your attackers are. In any case, you have to act quickly.

If you make a break for the transport,
turn to page 77.

If you try to find the mining tunnel,
turn to page 81.

You decide you'd better stay put as John has instructed. You look down at the bus and wonder why no one answers your calls. The bus continues its slow climb up the cliff face.

Minutes tick by. You take a sip from the nozzle in your helmet. The water-sucrose mix tastes horrible, but you can feel energy flow into your body.

The bus has almost reached the lip of the ledge. The clear blast-glass at the front should allow you to see into the control room and check that everyone is all right, but the sun's rays are shining directly on it; it's impossible to penetrate the glare. You turn the winch to the stop position and see the bus settle.

Maybe you should climb down to the air lock, you think. The air lock's operation is fairly simple, and you should be able to open it by yourself.

Just as you are about to start the precarious climb down, you see the air lock's outer door revolve to the closed position. Hopefully this means that someone is using it and not that a malfunction has caused it to lock. After a few more minutes, you see the air lock cycling again. You hold your breath until a suited figure carefully pulls itself from the doorway and looks around.

Turn to the next page.

"Up here! Up here!" you shout. But the figure does not turn toward you. You keep waving your arms and shouting until eventually the person does see you. Almost before you realize it, a shot from his or her cable gun has established a stable line on the ledge beside you. In only a few seconds, the figure is seemingly flying up toward you. Once he reaches you, you see by the face through the helmet's visor that it's one of the men you saw loading the bus earlier.

"What's going on here?" a voice says as the man touches his helmet to yours, a back-up way of communicating when radios are down. "We didn't know what was happening. The quake must have knocked out your radio. Are you all right?"

"Not really," you answer. "But right now John needs help badly. I think he was hit by some of the rocks on that upper ledge. Since my radio's broken, I have no idea if he's okay or not."

"That's bad news. I have to check to make sure the bus is secure first. Then I'll go check on John." Even as he says this, he starts to work the control panel of the winch. You see the bus move slowly and carefully back down the cliff.

Go on to the next page.

In a little while, you see more people struggle sideways out of the air lock. They seem to be trying to bring a stretcher with them. Four people use line guns to get to the ledge where John is. You hope he's not hurt. Then you feel the wooziness of delayed shock hit you like another quake. You pass out.

When you wake up, you see the bus at the bottom. There is no sign of the medical crew. The man who first came out of the air lock is shaking your shoulder. You see his lips moving but hear only silence.

"Time to get down to the bus," you hear as he remembers to lean down.

"What about John?" you ask.

"He'll be fine. He's sleeping right now."

You're barely aware of being taken down to the bus. Hurtling down a sheer cliff face with only a thin line to hold you doesn't even register as dangerous after the events of the day. Dr. Nasir is waiting for you inside the air lock, and she takes you to your sleeping berth. As soon as you lie down, you fall asleep again, but your dreams are full of falling rocks and exploding mountains. When you wake up hours later, you don't really feel refreshed, but at least the adrenaline from the excitement has worn off.

As you walk up the length of the bus, you see that John was not the only one hurt in the quake. The movement must have really shaken up the bus. A number of people are walking around with bandages and slings.

Turn to the next page.

76

"There you are," Dr. Nasir says behind you. "I was wondering if you were ever going to wake up. We have to make some new plans since this unforeseen circumstance has altered our original goals."

"What do you mean?"

"Well," she starts, "some people are going to go back in the emergency runners. With so many injuries, and John in such serious condition, we decided to cut the mission back. We're going to continue, but with just a bare-bones crew."

"Does that mean you want me to go back?" you ask.

"I think the decision should be up to you. Now you know just how dangerous these expeditions can be. If you do choose to continue, we will have plenty of work for you. With so many people hurt, every pair of hands will be invaluable."

"Let me think about it for a moment, I'm still a bit shaky," you tell her.

"Don't take too long. The emergency runner is leaving in twenty minutes, and they can't wait around unnecessarily."

If you choose to stay with the expedition despite the danger, turn to page 27.

If you decide to go back to Tycho with John to make sure he is all right, turn to page 126.

Another laser blast convinces you that you have to make your decision. You figure you have a better chance of escaping in the transport. You don't want to even think about Al's reaction if a delegate gets shot on your tour.

"Okay," you say over the broadcast frequency, "we're going to make a break for the transport." You grab the nearest delegate and point toward the transport. "We'll head out on the count of three."

You check to make sure that everyone understands the plan. There have been no more shots fired. You hope things stay that way. You have to move fast, and none of the Earthlings are skilled at moving in low gravity while wearing a no-pressure suit.

Turn to the next page.

"On the count of three," you repeat. "One . . . two . . . three!" At the drop of your third finger, everyone starts moving toward the transport. You feel as though a laser blast will puncture your suit any moment. But nothing happens.

Out on the plain you feel especially exposed, and that is when the sniper discovers you again. A blast of sand flies up in front of you. It's only a short distance to the transport, and you make it in a couple of long, low leaps. With no wasted movement, you get in and try to start the engine.

Three of your group have made it, and you feel hopeful until you see a delegate get hit in the back. She falls slowly to the floor of the crater. You hold your breath as two others lean down and struggle to pick up their fallen comrade: The telltale spray of dust around the back of the suit indicates that the delegate's air tanks have been hit.

You are the only one who knows how to deal with repressurizing a suit, but also the only one who can drive the transport. There is no way to know if the delegate is still alive, and if the rest of you are to survive, you have to get out of here fast.

If you decide to drive the transport to safety as quickly as possible, turn to page 91.

If you tell someone else to drive while you tend to the injured person, turn to page 111.

80

"I'm sorry," you say, "but I cannot do as you ask. My mind is my own. I understand your desire for longevity, but you have to realize that your culture is dead, and that living in my mind will not bring you back."

The image before you fades, but as it disappears, you hear one last message. "If you will not embrace us, then at least remember and honor us. We would do no less for you."

The next thing you know, you are standing with your hands and head pressed against the wall of the chamber. Dr. Nasir stands beside you, shaking you through your no-pressure suit and shouting into her radio. You try to gather your thoughts.

"Are you all right?" asks the doctor.

You feel dazed, and it's hard to stand. "Yes, I'm all right, but I need to sit down. Something very strange just happened."

"What? I came back here a few minutes ago and you were just staring at the wall."

"I think I just made the best decision for myself, but possibly the worst for humanity."

"I don't think you are all right," Dr. Nasir says carefully. "You don't sound like yourself."

"Well . . ." You don't really know what to tell her. You'll probably never be the same again.

You reach out to the wall. Before your glove touches the surface, the whole thing dissolves before you. A round hole appears again, but this time there are no flashing lights.

Turn to page 84.

You decide to try to escape through the mining tunnels. The problem is how to make it there with gun-toting thugs trying to kill you. You crawl over to one of the suited-up figures huddled on the ground and press your helmet to theirs, telling them your plan. Conveying information this way takes only a little while, but it feels like a century to you. Each second passing increases the likelihood of someone coming over the protective circle of rocks.

Finally you make a break for it. The main advantage you have is surprise. Even if the attackers know about the mining tunnels, you doubt that they will think to look for you there. The transport is the bigger target, so it will be more heavily guarded. The mining tunnels are in the opposite direction.

You feel extremely vulnerable as you crawl among the rocks. You have to lead the way. You hope everyone is following closely. Another laser blast hits the rocks, and more chips go flying, but it looks like the attackers are still aiming at the place where you were hiding. Sweat runs down your nose and forehead. The suit's cooling system is working overtime, but you can hardly tell the difference.

After ten minutes, you have gone about half a kilometer. You notice that the shooting has stopped. As you look behind to check how everyone is doing, you see something that fills you with hope and fear at the same time. The rocks above where you were have fallen down.

Turn to the next page.

If they figure you're still up there, they'll assume they have accomplished their task. You shiver at the thought. No one has ever tried to kill you before.

Who is doing this? you wonder. The Lunatic Fringe, a radical group that sprang up almost as soon as the colony was settled, has long advocated a free Luna, but they have always been committed to peaceful change.

Right now you have to focus on your immediate goals. As soon as you make it to the ridge, which is about two hundred meters away, you can start to move normally, and the entrance to the tunnel will be only a short distance farther. You continue to pull yourself carefully along. The urge to look back is strong, but you have to ignore it.

By the time you reach the ridge, you feel like you are going to explode. Every nerve along your spine is just waiting for the burning impact of a laser beam, but you make it over the lip and down the other side without anything happening. Now you have to wait for the others.

One by one, the delegates come crawling over the ridge. The looks on their faces tell you that they are just as nervous as you are. Once they are all over, you motion for them to follow you again. This time the going is much quicker, and you notice that the delegates are not making the simple mistakes they were just a short while before. Fear and desperation are helping everyone to really concentrate on what they are doing.

Turn to page 88.

When you look into the hole, all you can see is a clear globe. For a moment, the ghostlike glimmer of the alien's face appears faintly inside it. You realize the globe is the grave marker of an entire dead race. It is both beautiful and sad.

"I had a chance to keep them alive," you mutter.

"Nothing has been alive here for a very long time," says Dr. Nasir.

When you get back to the camp, you don't tell anyone about your experience. But in the weeks and years ahead, as you go about day-to-day life on Luna, strangers are drawn to you. They all want to talk about the same thing—their mysterious encounters with the beings who once called the Moon their home.

The End

You grab the med-kit from your waist, trying to move quickly without making any mistakes. You find the medical mini air lock located near the left carotid artery on John's neck. You take the stimulant ampoule out of its case, place it against the depression, and release the contents into his bloodstream.

"Come on, John! You can do it. Just wake up, and everything will be fine." John's life readings remain the same—steady, but not strong.

After what seems like centuries of waiting, you see John's lips move. You hear nothing, and his eyes are still closed, but you start to feel hopeful. He struggles to move, and you see a flash of pain twist his face. Suddenly his eyes open, and he stares straight at you.

Not knowing what else to do, you point to the jumble of fallen rocks and then over the ledge. John moves his head carefully to see, and you notice his mouth tighten. Crawling gingerly to the edge, he looks down at the winch and the bus.

Then John looks up and motions for you to bend down toward him. He moves upward until the clear blast-glass of your helmets meet. "Move me to the edge," he says. At first you are surprised at the sound of his voice. Then you realize that when the radios are down it's possible to communicate by touching helmets.

"Go easy, but if you have to, just pull me until you get me moving."

"Okay. Get ready."

Turn to the next page.

Moving John is a tough job, but not because of his weight. You could lift him with one arm, but you must be extra careful since you don't know how badly he's injured.

Once you reach the ledge, John tells you, "Give me the cable gun and set up the winch on this ledge so that it faces downward. Make sure that it's secure."

You do what he asks, although you can't imagine why he wants the winch set up.

John takes the cable gun in his hands and rests for a moment on the top of a rock. You see him wince each time he moves, but he keeps going with the same steady motions. Bracing himself, he aims the gun with delicate precision. He pulls the trigger and your eyes track the line as it hurtles downward.

The hook hits the direction lever square on. The metal bends at the impact, but the slipping appears to have halted. You smile as you turn to look at him. He looks happy and in pain at the same time. You lean down.

"Now all we have to do is get this winch down the slope and we'll be fine," John says. "First, tie the end of the cable around one of these big rocks and then rappel down with the winch over your shoulder. Then hook up the big cable, haul the bus up, and find out what's going on inside."

"Okay," you reply.

Go on to the next page.

Once you have completed this tricky maneuver, you have no time for self-congratulation. The inside of the bus is a mess. Gear is strewn about the interior, but the harnessed passengers seem to be okay.

After checking around, you find out that a flying scale knocked out one person, but other than that, everyone is just shaken up. You find Sarah strapped safely in her seat. She gives you a thumbs up and says, "Looks like you saved all our lives."

Dr. Nasir takes you aside and thanks you for saving everyone in the bus. You don't know how to reply, but you're happy nonetheless.

The End

88

In another ten minutes or so, you see the huge stone megalith that marks the entrance to the mine tunnels. When you were younger, your parents used to take you here on family outings, and that is when you found the tunnels. The massive rock stands over the entrance like a frozen gray soldier.

When you scramble down to the entrance, you are greeted by an unexpected development. A functioning, recently used air lock occupies the doorway. The last time you were here, the doorway was a simple hole leading deep into the heart of the moon. You wonder if you have discovered the home of your attackers.

You signal everyone forward and motion them to follow you through the air lock. As you wait for the air pressure to equal that of the interior, you try to figure out just what this place is.

Inside the tunnel is a room with two beds, chairs, a portable shower, and a camp kitchenette. What appears to be an extremely powerful bomb lies on the table. You wait for the others to come in before doing anything. Just looking at the bomb makes you nervous; the fact it's making a quiet clicking sound like a metronome hardly soothes your nerves.

Tools lie about the table. You hope this indicates that the bomb is not finished. You realize the situation is even more serious than you feared. A lone attacker is one thing, but an organized attempt is another. All you were supposed to do was give the delegates a tour of the colony, not get involved in some interplanetary plot.

Turn to the next page.

Most of the delegates have entered the room by now. You set off to explore the rest of your surroundings. Another air lock connects the apartment to the mining tunnels. By the time you get back to the entranceway, all the delegates are in the chamber, most of them staring at the bomb on the table.

"Well, we seem to have found the lair of our attacker," you say as you take your helmet off. "Now the question is, what do we do?"

"What do you mean?"

"Should we wait for the attacker to return and try to capture him—or them—or try to get back to the colony through the mine tunnels?"

"I'm no hero," says one of the delegates. "I think we should let the proper authorities handle this."

"I agree," you say. "But right now we're on our own, and unless we do something, or at least come up with a plan, all the authorities are going to be able to do is bury us."

"We see your point," another delegate finally says. "But you are more familiar with this type of situation than we are. You make the decision, and we'll follow your instructions."

If you decide to try to get back to the colony through the tunnels, turn to page 94.

If you choose to wait for the attackers to return, turn to page 122.

"Get in now!" you yell as you ready the transport engines.

As soon as the delegates carrying the injured person are halfway inside the transport, you gun the motor. No sound indicates the power you are releasing, but the vibrations almost shake you apart. Your spiked tires kick up a huge wave of Moon dust. You hope it will obscure the aim of your attacker. Even though you don't know how many are out there, you have to act as though you are surrounded. Nothing except rock protrusions shows up on your radar, but you know this doesn't mean anything. There are so many places to hide, even on the relatively flat surface of the crater, that radar is almost useless.

Turn to the next page.

92

Looking over your shoulder, you try to see how the injured person is doing. All you can see are a bunch of no-pressure suits huddled on the floor. Every time you turn, they all crash together. Since you are driving in zigzags, they crash a lot. "Take the emergency air bottles out of the starboard med-kit and screw them into the nozzle below the helmet," you call back. You can't tell if anyone is listening, and you have to keep your attention on your driving.

Go on to the next page.

In the distance you see the domes of the colony. Only a few more minutes, and you will reach the safety of the security zone. You wonder who would have attacked you. Clearly someone did not want the delegates from the Planetary Council to have a favorable opinion of the colony and its operation. Now that you have a little time to think, you realize your escape was easier than it should have been. All the attacker had to do was shoot the transport. After that he or she could have picked you off one by one.

Turn to page 98.

"I think we should try the tunnels," you say. "Getting you to safety is of primary importance. Once we get to the colony, we can let security deal with this situation." You begin to gather up the tools on the table near the bomb.

"What are you doing?" a delegate asks nervously.

"This may stop them from finishing the bomb," you answer. "If we're going to leave, we should get going. Five of you go down and get through the far air lock as quickly as you can. The rest of us will stay here and guard the door."

As you wait for the others to go through the air lock leading down to the mine tunnels, you finish collecting the tools spread along the table. Some are familiar, but others are completely alien to you. You shove them into a toolbox. Glancing at the two delegates guarding the door, you realize that with a few well-placed obstructions, you can block the air lock in the open position.

Air locks will not work if one of the doors is kept from closing properly. Rapid depressurization is at least messy, and at worst fatal. If you keep the assassins from getting in here, they will not be able to follow you or get to the bomb. Taking chisels and a hammer, you notch the metal all along the edge of the doorway. Then you and the two delegates jam as much furniture as possible in the doorway. Stepping back, you are pleased with your work. No one will be able to get through that air lock now.

Go on to the next page.

"Let's go," you tell the delegates. Taking the toolbox with you, you go down to the far air lock. Once through it, you put more notches into the door. Entering the tunnel, you wonder which way leads back to the colony. The beam of your helmet light pierces the darkness ahead of you.

As you travel through the tunnels, you mark each turn with a small cross etched into the wall. No one speaks, but everyone watches you intently. You travel along for hours, mostly in silence. You start to feel hungry, and you resist the urge to look at your watch. Each suit has enough air to last about eighteen hours.

"How much farther, do you think?" someone finally asks.

"Not much," you reply, but you know your answer isn't convincing. It's getting harder to breathe. When you look down at your air gauge, the level is lower than you had hoped. Trying not to think about it, you keep forging ahead through the tunnels.

Turn to the next page.

Just when you are ready to sit down and give up, you turn a corner and almost fall off the edge of a cliff. Your helmet light reveals a huge open space. The light is swallowed up before it reaches the other side. Looking down, you notice jagged rocks that eventually fade into black.

You take an emergency flare from your pouch, ignite the enclosed chemicals, and launch it into space. As you watch the flare fly down into the cavern, your hopes are ignited and quenched at the same time. You are in the main processing cavern. From here, you could easily make it to the colony's pressure tunnels. But you are over a kilometer above the floor, and the walls of the cliff are almost a straight vertical.

You try to remain calm. "This is the place we want to be," you tell the delegates. "The only problem is, we need to get down somehow."

"So what do we do?" asks a delegate.

"We can either try to climb down this cliff or go back into the tunnels and search for another route down. There definitely is one, but I'm not sure how to get to it."

If you decide to attempt the climb down, turn to page 119.

If you decide to look for another route to the cavern floor through the tunnels, turn to page 121.

A flash on the dashboard tells you that you are within radio range of the colony. "Mayday! Mayday!" you yell into the mouthpiece. "Delegates attacked and shot by unknown assailant. Require emergency medical attention now!"

"This is Commander Highbridge. What you are saying is impossible! Please identify yourself and get off official frequency. Over."

"Mayday! I repeat, Mayday! This is the tour guide. One of the delegates has been shot. Get a medical team here now!" The receiving area and the main air lock for transports are only a few hundred meters ahead. You keep the transport at maximum speed until the last instant.

As soon as you stop, you rush back into the main cabin and check on the person who was hit. One look is all you need to know that the medical personnel waiting on the other side of the air lock will be unnecessary. You slump against the wall of the transport.

When the investigation of the incident is over, you receive a commendation, but the attacker is never tracked down, and funding for the colony is sharply reduced.

The End

Distracted by the popping noise and the revelation that there is an atmosphere inside this room, you do not notice at first the new hole in the floor that reveals thousands of blinking lights and moving machinery. The hole is over two meters wide and goes down farther than you can see. Somehow you doubt that Dr. Nasir went this way. Maybe you should go back in the other direction. But when you turn around, the opening you came through is gone.

Suddenly, before you realize what is happening, a metal tentacle writhes out of the hole and grabs your legs. With a jerk, you are pulled forward. Your head bangs against the hard floor, and even through your helmet you feel dazed. You're pulled into the hole, where more tentacles snake out from the sides and wrap you in their grip.

Turn to the next page.

100

"Help!" you scream, but you get no reply.

You struggle to get free, but you have nothing to use for leverage, and all you can manage is to wiggle around a bit. The space below you is filled with the mass of tentacles, but you can tell that the hole is deep—you cannot see the bottom. A blue light pulses every now and then, and when it hits your eyes you start to feel weak and nauseous. As you continue to struggle, the tentacles start to wrap themselves around your helmet.

Time loses meaning as you struggle helplessly in the hole. You are being sucked down toward the blue light. Suddenly you realize that you are going to be this thing's next meal!

One of the tentacles has tightened around your helmet. As it continues to squeeze, small cracks appear in the visor, and your stomach churns. Another tentacle begins to poke its way through the cracked glass. The tentacle has a sharp point, and it moves slowly into your helmet, toward your face. With tremendous effort you try to break free of the tentacles, but you're trapped. In a final act of desperation, you spit at your enemy.

When your spit hits the probe, you hear a sizzling sound. The probe thrashes about spastically, as if in pain. It lunges toward your face, and not knowing what else to do, you spit again. This time the sizzling sound is combined with an intense flash of blue light. Dizziness overcomes you, and you lose consciousness.

Turn to the next page.

102

When you wake up, the probe is gone. You see the small hole in your helmet visor. Panic seizes you; a hole means death most of the time. It takes you a moment to realize that if there had been no atmosphere, you would have never regained consciousness. The tentacles are still holding you.

Spitting definitely repelled the probe, but you don't know why. If it was the chemical nature of human spit, you have no hope. Even spitting all day, you would never be able to overcome all the tentacles. You have to hope it was water that made the probe react that way.

Taking a look at your control panels, you see that you have more than a liter of water in your tank. The water is meant for drinking, but you are more concerned with your escape than your possible thirst. As you check your control panels, you realize how frozen with panic you've been. Your emergency distress beacon hasn't even been activated. Just as you are about to flip the switch, you take a look at your power levels. If you use the beacon, you won't have enough power in your suit to make the sealer work on the hole in your helmet. If you want to get free by using the water in your tank, you will have to make another hole. You have to decide between trying to free yourself or calling for someone to rescue you.

---

*If you try to break free by yourself,
turn to page 103.*

*If you use your remaining power on the
distress beacon, turn to page 39.*

Even though all the emergency guidelines recommend using your distress beacon, you have the feeling this situation demands more active control. Besides, waiting passively while caught in the grasp of these tentacles is just too counterintuitive for you, and you have no guarantee that the probe won't return with a new, waterproof covering.

You glance down at your water supply, then grab the tube in your teeth and suck up a mouthful of water. Opening your lips, you push your tongue up and forward against your tightly clenched teeth. A stream of water shoots through the small gap in your front teeth. At first you miss the hole, but you quickly redirect the stream. Once again you hear a sizzling sound, and the tentacles wrapped around your helmet begin to writhe and squirm. With a quick pause for more water, you aim out the hole again. By the time your mouth runs dry, most of the tentacles are gone from the helmet, and you can turn your head again. This is what you were hoping for.

Moving your head to the right, you suck up another mouthful and aim at your right arm. As soon as the water hits the tentacles there, they let go and whip about as if in pain. One smashes against your midsection. You think one of your ribs might be broken, but you keep on spraying water. The gauge tells you that half your water is gone.

Turn to page 123.

You tell the alien you will accept the offer.

"Very well then, I believe you have made the correct choice. Be forewarned. The assimilation process will be disorienting."

"Okay. But make it quick, or I might change my mind," you say, trying not to think about what you're agreeing to.

"Thank you," the image says. Then he disappears. The inside of your head becomes a jumble of colors and sensations. You can't tell if one hour or one century passes as you live and experience the lives of the aliens. You cry for their pain and misunderstandings, but also experience the love they felt. Some of what happens is incomprehensible to you at first, but as you are wrapped in the experiences of a whole race, you gain insight into the dreams and fears that caused them to behave in their own particular way.

The aliens, who thought of themselves as the Chan-a-Larra, or the People Who Dream, placed tremendous importance on the ability to draw others into their thoughts. The closest human equivalent would be telepathy. You realize this is what happened when you were talking to the alien being. The Chan-a-Larra did not see with their eyes the way humans do, but they did absorb wavelengths of electromagnetic radiation through their bodies. Some of the art they created reached levels of complexity you could never have imagined. But they also used their gifts for torture and war.

Turn to the next page.

106

After a time, the thoughts and experiences of the Chan-a-Larra recede a little. You feel full of their knowledge. Not only are you aware of what they did, you also know how to do it yourself. Without having to test your ability, you know that you can bring all of humanity into your dream. No single Chan-a-Larra would have been able to do this.

Go on to the next page.

You know that you now have the power to stop all human pain and misunderstanding. By bringing others into your dream, you can make people reject war and prejudice. Peace will become the natural state.

"Do I have the right to make people do what I want?" you ask yourself.

You realize that you are back in your body. When you look at the clock in the display panel of your helmet, you are surprised to see that only fifteen minutes have passed since Dr. Nasir left you in this room. In that time you have aged millions of years. You know the feelings and thoughts of countless others. Even in their alien-ness, they were much like humans. The one thing you do not know is why they died.

The only life they have left is now within you. With the technology they possessed, you could help create a golden age of plenty. No one would go hungry, and people would be freed from crushing pain and work. But you would have to bring everyone into the dream of peace. The memory of how that technology was warped to inflict pain and suffering is strong.

"Would people want me to give them this kind of peace and security?"

If you decide that bringing others into your dream is the only way to stop war and suffering, turn to page 108.

If you decide you do not have the right to make people do what you want them to, turn to page 68.

108

Holding the knowledge of the dream firmly in your mind, you sit and weave your way into the world of the unconscious. As you drift beyond the realm of the living and the thinking, you open yourself up to feeling and emotion. Using extreme care, you build an image of humanity as it should be. You try not to take away the free will that has grown so vital to humankind. At the same time, you try to construct a reality where violence becomes not only impossible but also unthinkable.

Each step shows you more. You realize how deeply the urge for violence goes, but you carefully track the taint down to its roots and make sure it will not be possible to revitalize such thoughts. Awareness of other human minds comes to you, and you see the changes that have already taken place. Even within yourself you notice how your thoughts about force have been altered. Ideas like greed, fear, and vengeance are extinguished from your mind until they exist only as arcane concepts, not as possibilities.

Go on to the next page.

There is resistance to your dream, but you reach out with even more power and subtlety. Some minds resist, while others embrace your dream as if they had always thought it to be true. You feel the thoughts of all humanity, and you see how those thoughts are growing closer and closer to harmony.

Ideas come into your head and then spread out with the speed of thought. The flow is not a one-way channel though, and once again, a flood of emotions and memories engulfs you. This time the experiences are human. Each mind forms its own unique structure in the composite whole, and you feel a consciousness forming that goes beyond the individual.

Turn to the next page.

110

You can't tell how long it took to complete the process of sending and receiving thoughts, but when it's finally over you feel a momentary peace. You look around you and realize you're still standing in the same room, as if nothing has changed. Will the passing on of the dream succeed and help to save humanity? Or are humans doomed to extinction, just like the alien race that went before you?

These thoughts exhaust you. You become dizzy and you have the sensation of becoming one with the universe, conquering time and space. It all becomes a blur until you regain your focus, conscious that eons of time have passed.

"Do not be afraid," you say to the startled presence before you. "I am the essence of the dead human race. We have been dust for longer than you would believe, and we desire to have someone to know and remember us."

"What do you mean?"

"We attempted too much, and the cost was stagnation and death. The knowledge I will pass on to you originated with the very first life forms that existed in the Universe. It has been passed on from one extinct race of beings to another. It will help you avoid the fate of all who have gone before you if you use it correctly."

"What do you want from me?"

"Nothing, except for someone to know who we are and what we did. Someone to know the dangers of the path of power. We failed, but you do not have to."

The End

Does anyone know how to drive a big machine?" you call out to the delegates.

"I drove a combine tractor on a farm back home," a petite woman answers. "But it looked nothing like this."

"You're the driver," you say. You attach emergency air supplies to the shot delegate. "The big white lever is the throttle, and the big red lever is the braking system. The pedal on the floor is the clutch. Now move!" As quickly as you get new air into the damaged suit, it leaks out again. It is the female delegate from North America who has been shot.

Go on to the next page.

112

Turning her over, you look at where she was hit. Metal and plastic are fused together, and her suit has been punctured in at least three places. She's been knocked unconscious, but she doesn't seem to be hurt. However, her lips are already turning blue, and if she goes much longer without fresh air, she may die.

The transport lurches into motion. You are caught off guard and slam into the back wall. Without your suit, you would have been crushed. As it is, you feel dazed, but your crash was not without benefit. You have knocked one of the bulkhead compartments open, and what you see inside makes your brain work overtime.

"Emergency sealant foam," reads the container in the bulkhead. It is meant for repairs of the transport, but you figure that it's the only thing you've got that may reseal the delegate's torn suit. You quickly read the instructions on the container.

Go on to the next page.

The air bottle you just attached is nearly empty. You get ready to spray the punctured suit with sealant. You release the nozzle and squeeze the trigger. A fine white spray shoots from the nozzle's end. As soon as it comes in contact with the ruptured suit, it congeals into a foamy mass. Even after the back of the suit is covered, you keep spraying the sealant until the container is empty.

"Is she going to be okay?" the delegate from Asia asks.

"I'm not sure," you answer. "But I don't really have any more time to tend to her. Did you see how I attached the air bottle to the front of her suit?" The man nods. "Good. Take this bottle and attach it. I'm going up to the cabin to see what's going on outside."

Turn to the next page.

"I hope she makes it," the man says.

"We've got a long way to go yet," you reply. "I'm afraid that last knock we took might have damaged something. I don't like the way we're moving."

Carefully you make your way to the front of the transport. You feel a deep vibration that makes you nervous. Once inside the control cabin, you glance at your driver. She is biting her lower lip, but her movements are decisive and sure. You're not sure you would have done as good a job if the situation were reversed.

Go on to the next page.

"How are you doing?" you ask.

"Not bad, but I think there's something wrong with the steering. It's getting harder and harder to turn."

"I thought as much," you say as you point to the hydraulic-fluid gauge. The gauge is below the halfway mark, and you can see the needle drop as you watch.

"What does that mean?" the driver asks you.

"We have to aim the transport toward the colony and hope we get close enough to walk or call for help."

"Why not call for help now?" she asks.

"Because whoever shot at us is a lot closer than the colony, and they would be able to determine our position. Here, let me take over. You've done a great job, but I'm sure you're exhausted."

As you drive, the steering becomes more and more difficult to control. After a while, you decide to hike the remaining distance to the colony on foot. Before you abandon the transport, you make a distress call to the colony. Even if the attackers overhear, your chance of being rescued will be much greater if someone knows to look for you.

Turn to the next page.

The injured delegate has to be carried. You don't like the readings on her life monitors, but you try to be optimistic for everyone else's sake. Deep down, though, you are really scared. As you move on, you realize you are too far away from the colony to make it on the air left in your tanks. You are thinking about this when you see another transport heading toward you. At first you're worried that it's the attackers, but the transport is coming from the direction of the colony and has the official symbol of the Protectors. Waving your arms, jumping up and down, and shouting into your radio, you manage to attract their attention. The transport pulls up to your group, and before you can do anything, two soldiers with guns jump out.

"Good thing we found you," says one of the soldiers. "Apparently the assassins we sent out didn't do the job. I guess we'll have to finish you off ourselves."

The soldiers raise their guns. You close your eyes, not wanting to see the betrayed looks on the delegates' faces.

The Lunar government's assassination of the Planetary Council delegates causes an interplanetary war of immense proportion. The peaceful life you knew on Luna becomes just a distant memory.

The End

"Does anyone here know how to rock climb?" you ask. "No? Well, neither do I. Since we don't have any rope, everyone will be on their own. Remember, a fall from this height in low gravity is not as bad as on Earth, but it could still be fatal. Be careful."

Taking a deep breath, you peer over the edge and prepare to work your way down. The going is slow, and many times you almost slip, but at least there are plenty of handholds. You start to get more confident. When you look up, the others seem to be doing all right.

After three hours of slow progress, you are ready to scream. Your legs and arms are shaky and burning with pain, but you have to keep going. Looking down, you gauge that the floor of the cavern is about two-thirds closer; your helmet light actually reaches it. That's when you look up to see a body flying down at you. The suited figure is twisting in the air, occasionally hitting the rock wall. As the person comes near you, you reach out and try to grab an arm or leg. You miss and lose your grasp on the wall. You bounce the rest of the way to the floor.

Incredibly, you don't think you're injured. You look over and see the person who fell. With relief you see that the figure wiggles its arms and legs. Closing your eyes, you wait for the others to get down. Once they do, you will guide them back to the colony and turn these delegates over to someone else. You decide you have had enough of leading tours for the rest of your life.

The End

Once inside the plant, you can tell the delegates are very impressed. The gleaming equipment looks mysterious and advanced, even though you aren't sure what it's for. The most impressive demonstration is the actual refining of the different chemicals and compounds that are produced. To extract various chemicals from one another, a row of high-powered lasers carefully excite the compounds and determine their composition. After the analysis, the twisted lumps of material are dropped into baths of different solutions. The resulting explosions are dramatic, and you're sure you're not the only one who is thankful for the meter-thick glass shielding.

"Before we leave the facility, we will show you the banks of supercomputers responsible for calculating these very precise processes," says the guard.

As you open the door to the computer labs, you see the delegate from Garania smile in triumph, reaching inside his pouch. Reacting instantly, you charge him. Your momentum knocks him to the ground and the pouch skitters across the floor. You rush to it and open the flap. A set of whirring numbers in a countdown to zero flash before your vision. The last image you ever see, before the white flash of the bomb's explosion, is a small screen that reads 00:01.

The End

"No sense in trying to make it down if we die in the process," you say. "If we can't find another way to the bottom, we can always come back and make a try for it."

Even though the others accept your decision, going back into the tunnels is one of the hardest things you have ever done. To be so close to freedom and yet know that death might be its price makes your task much harder.

As you work your way backward, you try to sense which direction will take you toward the floor. But every time you take a tunnel that seems to lead down, it backs around on itself and ends up going upward. You continue to make scratches on the walls as you turn. But before too long, you have no idea where you are. You find you're making scratches on the same walls, locked in an infernal loop. Your breath is labored now, and not just from all the exercise you have gotten.

"All right," you announce, "this is getting us nowhere. Let's use those spare bottles to refresh ourselves and go back and try to climb down that cliff." There is no real response to your words except a slow shuffling of feet as people turn around.

Going back, you make better time as you retrace your steps. But then the trail becomes suddenly unfamiliar. You scurry back and forth, but the path only seems more and more confused. Your thoughts become muddled as your oxygen begins to run out.

When the miners find you, it is too late.

The End

"I only have a vague idea of how the tunnels connect," you say. "Let's try to catch the assassin off guard. We should be able to surprise him. Even if there's more than one person, each has to go through the air lock independently." You can see that after being shot at and almost buried, you aren't the only one who wants revenge.

"What should we do?" the South American delegate asks.

"First, does anyone know anything about bombs?" Your only answer is the shaking of seven heads. You take a deep breath. "Okay, then let's have two people guard the door while the rest of us get out of our no-pressure suits. We'll have greater mobility that way." You reach for a sheet from one of the cots and address two of the delegates. "Here, take this bedsheet and be prepared to cover whoever comes through the air lock. If he can't see, he'll be at a disadvantage. He'll probably be carrying a laser rifle, but hopefully he'll be cautious about using it around the bomb."

As you look around the room, you notice an emergency med-kit for mining operations that contains a suit hypodermic. No-pressure suits on Luna are designed with a special seal under the helmet joint for hypodermic injections. Each med-kit contains a general anesthetic. You hurry to make the preparations.

Turn to page 124.

Now that your arm is free, you can open the water line directly. Over half the water that you tried to spray through the hole in your helmet is leaking down your suit. You search for the mini-laser drill in the supply pouch on your waist. Taking it out, you aim it at one of the tentacles. Nothing happens.

The air and water supply lines for your suit are gathered together and pass in a bunch under your belt. You take the blue water line out and carefully aim the laser drill at it.

The blue tube is sliced in half. Water begins to spurt out. Aiming the tube as best you can, you spray water over all the tentacles you see. Immediately everything becomes chaos. When the tentacles stop writhing, you are hanging by your left hand in a hole.

Crawling down the side of the hole in the direction of the fading blue light, you wait for the tentacles to come alive at any moment. You've tied your water tube in a slipknot for easy access in case of another attack, but you make it to the bottom without any more alien activity. Once there, you see that the floor of the hole is translucent. Through it you can make out the surface of the Moon. The gray wasteland has never looked so good to you. You patch the holes in your suit with the last of your power.

Now all you have to do is get one of the skimmer crafts, bring back some water tanks and hoses, and go looking for the doctor. You wonder if anyone will believe what happened to you until they see this place for themselves.

The End

124

"As soon as one of the attackers comes through the air lock," you say, "and you two have blinded him, I'll inject him. Hopefully everything will be over quickly." You motion for someone to hold the syringe while you get out of your suit.

Then you wait. More than an hour goes by. Finally the in-use light on the air lock lights up. As soon as the door slides open, two delegates wrap a startled figure in the sheet. You rush forward, but as you do so, the blinded figure punches out randomly and cracks you in the head. Everything goes into slow motion.

Watching the needle fly through the air, you know that this is the end. If the intruder can get that rifle going, he'll overpower the eight of you quickly. You see the delegate from Garania scramble for the syringe and rush to the sheet-covered figure. In one sure motion, he pushes the needle through the special seal. At first nothing happens, but then the attacker stops fighting and collapses beside you.

You try to cheer, but all you manage is a weak grunt. By the time the SOS you send out is answered, all you care about is getting home. Al better give you a big bonus for this tour.

The End

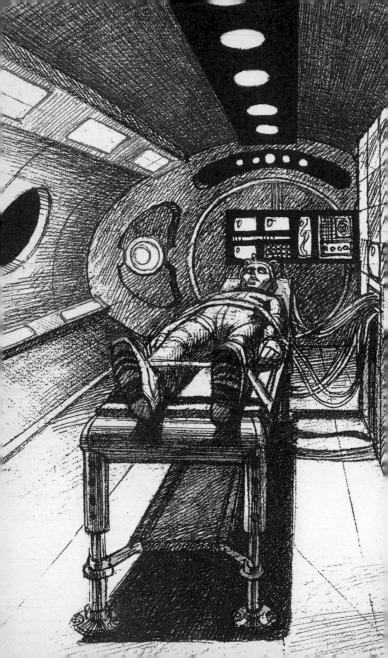

The emergency runner is crowded with the wounded and their caregivers, so you try to remain as unobtrusive as possible. Every now and then you check the life meters connected to John. He seems to just be sleeping, with nothing immediately apparent to indicate that he is severely wounded, but all the monitors are flashing yellow lights.

Since the runner is meant as an emergency vehicle, it consists of engines and little else. Instead of seats you have to strap yourself to the metal floor, and the noise inside the cabin is tremendous. Still, you are very thankful to be here at all. You hate to think what would have happened if you couldn't get John to the hospital.

The transport speeds across the plain. Every time it hits a rock, the runner goes flying. Each bump makes you worry more about John, but his readings stay pretty much the same.

After an hour or so of being bumped around, you finally spot Tycho in the distance. One of John's lights goes into the red scale, and you notice that the med staff looks concerned. "You can make it, John. Just a little farther," you say.

Turn to the next page.

By the time you reach the city, three of John's life-support readings are red. As soon as the runner stops, a crew from the hospital swarms aboard and takes all the wounded away. You are left to yourself, and you're not really sure what you should do, so you head home. Your parents are surprised to see you, but you're too drained to answer their questions.

You call the hospital to see if John is okay. They put you on hold, and you start to realize that you did not escape completely unscathed from the quake. Bruises cover your arms. But then you hear a voice that makes you forget your pain.

"Yes, it seems we got him here in time. He is still in critical condition, but we expect a full recovery. He owes you his life."

"Thanks . . . thanks a lot," you say, before hanging up the phone and going to bed.

The End

CREDITS

Illustrator: Vladimir Semionov was born in August 1964 in the Republic of Moldavia, of the former USSR. He is a graduate of the Fine Arts Collegium in Kishinev, Moldavia as well as the Fine Arts Academy of Romania, where he majored in graphics and painting. He has had exhibitions all over the world, in places like Japan and Switzerland, and is currently art director of the SEM&BL Animacompany animation studio in Bucharest.

This book was brought to life by a great group of people:

Shannon Gilligan, Publisher

Gordon Troy, General Counsel

Jason Gellar, Sales Director

Melissa Bounty, Senior Editor

Stacey Boyd, Designer

Thanks to everyone involved!

ABOUT THE AUTHOR

Anson Montgomery lives in Warren, Vermont with his wife, Rebecca, and his two daughters, Avery and Lila. He went to the Groton School and Williams College. Anson enjoys skiing, mountain biking, hiking, reading, and chess. The Moon, and space exploration in general, have always been of interest to him.

For games, activities and other fun stuff, or to write to Anson Montgomery, visit us online at CYOA.com

Introduces

The Golden Path

A three-book interactive epic story.
There is more than one way to get
from one book to the next,
but only one Golden Path.

FROM: Dianna Torman
dtorman@deadmail.anonymous.guyana.000
SUBJECT: Something has happened to us.

Sweetheart, I don't want to alarm you, but I fear I must. If you are getting this email it is because something has happened to us. It is rigged to be sent from a special "dead drop" anonymous server if I have not checked back in three days. Your father and I have been afraid that people were moving against us after we were removed from heading the Carlsbad dig. I can't get too specific because I do not know myself who exactly is targeting us. We will try and contact you as soon as we are able.

Leave school and go see your Uncle Harry in Carlsbad. He works in the branch office of the Federal Historical Accuracy Board and he can help you. His work address is: FHAB District Office, Harold Turner, 224 Mesa Street, Suite B11, Carlsbad, NM.

Don't call him or email him, just go see him as soon as possible!

Use the flyer at home if you can. It has enough fuel to get to Carlsbad, and its transponder codes have been authorized to fly there. Don't try going anywhere else though, as the Gatekeepers will immediately stop you. They keep a tight leash on all flyers.

Rimy can give you a ride home from school; he is a trusted friend. Just tell him I asked him as a "special boon."

I will try and leave a more detailed note in the secret spot. There is much your father and I need to explain to you, but I can't really explain until I see you in person. I can't wait until I see your beautiful face! Be strong, be brave, and know that your father and I love you more than life itself! I am sorry to scare you with this news, but it will all work out in the end!!!!

Love,
Mom

"I think I'm going to be sick," you moan as soon as you finish your mom's email. Maybe this is just some big joke? But Tito's death is no joke, and nothing about this day has been very funny. "I don't even have an 'Uncle Harry.'"

The phone rings and all three of you jump. You look at the caller ID, and it says: Billings, Palmer and Polk.

"It's my parents' financial advisor. He calls all the time, but why would he be calling at midnight?"

"Hello?" you say into the mouthpiece.

"It's Preston Billings here, are your parents home? I need to talk to Dianna or Donald immediately."

"No, Mr. Billings, they're not here. I don't know where they are. I think they are in trouble." Billings has always been nice to you, but you don't know why you tell him that.

"What do you mean in trouble?" he asks. "They were on their way to meet me here tonight. In New York City. But they never showed up. God! I hate that they outlawed cell phones. All for safety!" He gives a bitter laugh.

"Why were they coming to meet you?" you ask.

"I think it would be best if you came here to New York City. I have some new information for your parents that is very important to all of you."

"I think someone has taken them," you say weakly, voicing your fear for the first time. "We found my mom's dog Tito dead in their workshop. The house is...neat but everything just seems strange."

There's a long pause.

"Honestly, I think you need to get out of there right now," Mr. Billings says urgently. "I can arrange a travel document via email. Do you have a car?"

"Yes," you answer. Peter and Dresdale are staring at you with intense eagerness, but they are keeping silent and following your lead. You haven't mentioned them yet. "Mr. Billings, I am not sure

I should tell you this, but my mom sent an email that would only be triggered if they were in trouble. I just read it. She says I need to go meet with someone in Calsbad, some friend of theirs."

"Don't go to Carlsbad!" he says. "Not with the explosion. It's is too dangerous now! Listen, give me your email address and I'll send the travel documents in the morning. Right now I want you to get out of there."

"Why?" you ask. You have a flashback to that afternoon when you first saw the tall figure of Dr. Schlieman.

"I really can't talk over the phone," Billings replies. "Please take my word for it. I'll email you the documents. Get out of there as quickly as possible."

The phone line goes dead.

You are stunned. Things seem to be moving fast, and in the wrong direction. You look at your two friends.

"What do we do? This flyer your mom mentioned in her email, how did they get it?" Peter asks.

"The government gave them a low level flyer for the excavation they did in Belize. They didn't use it much at the Carlsbad dig. It should fit the three of us with room for half a toothbrush."

"What did that Billings guy say?" Dresdale asks.

"He said we should get out of here as soon as possible and go to New York City to meet him. He says he has information for my parents. They were scheduled to be there to meet him tonight. He also said 'don't go to Carlsbad.'" Your head pulses with a weary ache, but your heart and stomach feel much worse

"I hate to say this, but I am going to faint if I don't get some food," says Peter. Dresdale glares at him. "What?" he asks defensively. "I haven't eaten since we had mac and cheese at the dining hall for lunch."

"No, you're right. We need to get some food, and get out of here," you say. "But where do we go?"

"Can you operate the flyer?" Dresdale asks.

"It's mostly automated, but my dad let me take it into manual mode a couple of times. You don't get very high off the ground and if the power quits it has a backup elevation field that brings you down easy. Where do you guys think I should go?"

"What do you mean, 'I'?" says Dresdale. "We're coming with you."

"Yeah," agrees Peter. "But after we get some food!"

"These are my problems. You two should go to Dresdale's Mom's house" you reply. "I've gotten you in enough trouble. I'll take care of this."

"Don't be nuts. We're not going to let you go off by yourself. Anyway, I'm not sure what is going on, but somehow I think that we are all in this together," Dresdale says, and her face looks so earnest and caring that you feel almost good for a second. Then reality comes crashing down again.

"So where are we going? Do we listen to the email from my mom and take the flyer or listen to Billings and go to the Big Soggy Apple?"

If you choose to follow your mother's plea in the dead-drop email and go to Carlsbad to meet "Uncle Harry", turn to page 43.

If your gut tells you to go to New York City to meet Preston Billings and learn his "important information", turn to page 36.